ISBN 0 86037 398 3

MUSLIM CHILDREN'S LIBRARY

HILMY THE HIPPO SERIES

HILMY THE HIPPO
Learns About Vanity

Author *Rae Norridge*
Illustrator *Leigh Norridge Marucchi*
Designer *Nasir Cadir*
Co-ordinator *Anwar Cara*

Published by
The Islamic Foundation
Markfield Conference Centre
Ratby Lane, Markfield
Leicester LE67 9SY
United Kingdom

T (01530) 244 944
F (01530) 244 946
E i.foundation@islamic-foundation.org.uk
     publications@islamic-foundation.com

Quran House, PO Box 30611, Nairobi, Kenya

PMB 3193, Kano, Nigeria

British Library Cataloguing in Publication Data

Norridge, Rae
   Hilmy the hippo learns about vanity
   1. Hilmy the Hippo (Fictitious character) - Pictorial works
   - Juvenile fiction 2. Pride and vanity - Pictorial works -
   Juvenile fiction 3. Children's stories - Pictorial works
   I. Title
   823.9'2 [J]

ISBN 0860373983

HILMY THE HIPPO

Rae Norridge

Learns About Vanity

Illustrated by *Leigh Norridge Marucchi*

THE ISLAMIC FOUNDATION

One bright, sunny morning Hilmy splashed about in his water hole. The birds were singing in the nearby trees and the blue dragonfly was sunning himself, his wings outstretched, on a water lily leaf.

Hilmy saw a flash of green and bright scarlet as a beautiful bird flew by. He had never seen this bird before. *Subhanallah*, this is truly a magnificent bird, thought Hilmy. I wonder where it lives?

Hilmy hurriedly left the water and ran over to the tree in which the beautiful bird had perched. As Hilmy approached, the bird flew on to another tree. Hilmy followed.

"*As-Salamu 'Alaykum*," called the sparrow, who was watching Hilmy running from tree to tree. "What are you doing, Hilmy?"

"*Wa 'Alaykum as-Salam*," replied Hilmy. "I have seen the most beautiful bird. It is a lovely shade of green with wings of scarlet. Do you know where it lives, Sparrow?"

The sparrow chuckled. "Yes, it is the Lourie bird. It lives in the thick forest that covers the floor of the valley."

"Thank you, Sparrow," said Hilmy and hurriedly went on his way.

5

If such a beautiful bird lives in the forest, surely there must be other creatures just as beautiful, thought Hilmy. Creatures I have never seen before. I think I will go and see for myself. And besides, I have never been to the forest.

When Hilmy reached the forest, he saw the Lourie bird, flashing its scarlet wings as it flitted from branch to branch. When Hilmy drew near, the bird took flight. Hilmy followed.

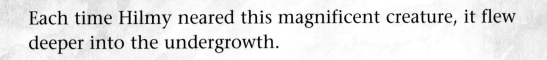

Each time Hilmy neared this magnificent creature, it flew deeper into the undergrowth.

Soon Hilmy came to a clearing. Bright sunshine fell onto a pool of clear water. Hilmy was now very thirsty, so he walked over to the pool to drink. But as he bent his head over the water, he saw his reflection.

Hilmy gasped, as he had never seen his reflection before. I am such a fine looking hippo, he said to himself, in fact I am a very handsome hippo.

I am the handsomest hippo I have ever seen. He opened his mouth and examined his teeth. Hmm, thought Hilmy, I have never seen such beautiful teeth. It is so nice to look at myself. The water in my water hole is always muddied with everyone drinking from it.

The following day Hilmy returned to the forest to find the clear pool in which he could see his reflection. I am so beautiful; perhaps I should live in the forest, thought Hilmy. All the beautiful creatures live in the forest. He had seen the bushbuck with its beautiful chestnut coat and big brown eyes. It too, was truly a magnificent animal.

Day after day Hilmy returned to the pool,
and day after day, he admired his reflection.

But one morning when Hilmy set out for the forest, grey
clouds had begun to gather in the sky overhead. He hurried
on his way, eager to get to the forest as quickly as he could.
He ran through the trees and found the clearing where the
pool lay. He leaned over the water and admired his beauty.

Suddenly his reflection was shattered by a single raindrop. "My face," cried Hilmy, "it's falling to pieces."

He looked up and saw the beautiful Lourie bird.

"Tell me Lourie bird. Please tell me that my face is not shattered," sobbed Hilmy.

The Lourie bird laughed and said, "No Hilmy, it's only the rain that has broken your reflection."

Hilmy looked up at the sky and saw the rain falling from the clouds. "Go away," he shouted angrily. "Go away rain. You have spoilt my beautiful reflection. Go away and never come back."

The Lourie bird heard Hilmy shouting. "Hilmy," said the bird, "Do you know what will happen if the rain did go away, and it never came back?"

"I don't care," cried Hilmy. "I like to look at myself. After all, I am very handsome."

The Lourie bird was very angry with Hilmy. He spread his beautiful scarlet wings and flew away.

Insha' Allah, thought Hilmy, tomorrow the rain would've stopped and I can once again see how beautiful I am.

On his way back to his water hole he met Stripe the zebra.

"You look very sad Hilmy," said Stripe. "Is there something wrong?"

"Yes, Stripe," replied Hilmy angrily. "The rain is falling and I cannot admire myself in the pool of clear water. I want the rain to stop and never come back."

"But Hilmy," said Stripe. "Allah sends the rain so that everything can grow and we can have water to drink. We must thank Allah for giving us rain."

"We have enough water in the rivers, and everything is growing," retorted Hilmy as he hurried on his way.

He met a family of hyenas. They were rolling in the mud and enjoying themselves. What ugly creatures, thought Hilmy.

"Hilmy, come and join us," called Mother Hyena, with mud clinging to her cheeks. "It is such fun to splash about in the mud. *Al-Hamdulillah*, it is wonderful that Allah has sent the rain."

16

Hilmy ignored Mother Hyena. She is too ugly for the likes of me. I am too handsome to talk to her, thought Hilmy and hurried on his way.

When Hilmy reached his water hole he saw Giant, the big elephant, drinking from the water. The rain splashed down, covering everything in raindrops.

"*As-Salamu 'Alaykum*, Giant," called Hilmy. "I wish this rain would go away."

"*Wa 'Alaykum as-Salam*," replied the elephant raising his majestic head.

"Hilmy, the rain is life giving. Why do you want it to go away?"

"It has broken my reflection," replied Hilmy. "I cannot see myself in the pool when it is raining. I am beautiful and I like to look at myself."

The mighty elephant turned to Hilmy and said, "If the rain went away, the grass and the trees would die."

19

Hilmy looked at the elephant with a defiant look in his eyes and replied,

"Does it matter? I can eat the reeds in the river. I do not need the grass. I do not need the trees. I like to look at my reflection and the silly rain spoilt it all."

"But Hilmy," replied Giant. "If it does not rain the rivers will dry up and there will be no reeds for you to eat. Fish and other creatures that depend on the rivers will also die. You are a hippo, and hippos need the rivers.

If the grass and the trees die, so will many creatures, as
they depend on the trees and the grass for their survival.
All Allah's creatures would have nothing to drink. You
want the rain to go away all because of your vanity."

"What is vanity?" asked Hilmy.

"Vanity is self-praising, Hilmy. It is when someone admires
himself too much. And that is what you have been doing
when you see your own reflection.

21

You do not have to look at your reflection in the pool to know that you are beautiful. Allah created all creatures, therefore all creatures are beautiful. The leaf that shivers in the wind is beautiful, because Allah created it. Every grain of sand that sparkles so brightly is beautiful, because it is Allah's creation.

Every flower, every bird, every raindrop is beautiful. Yet they do not need their reflection to tell them so, they know they are beautiful, because Allah created them."

Hilmy looked at Giant. He was truly a majestic creature. So large and powerful, yet, so silent and gentle.

The sun came out and Hilmy sniffed the air. It smelt so clean and fresh. Yes, thought Hilmy, the rain is good. All the creatures will be pleased that it has rained because the rain gives life to everything. Even I would have suffered if it did not rain. I have been foolish.

23

"Vanity is a selfish thing Hilmy," continued the wise elephant. "We must never believe that we are more beautiful than the next. We are all equal, because Allah made it so."

"*Jazak Allah*, Giant," said Hilmy as he watched the elephant walk away. "I know now that from the tiniest insect to the mighty elephant, we are all beautiful creations of Allah. *Astagfirullah*, I will never be vain again."

GLOSSARY
of Islamic Terms

As-Salamu 'Alaykum
Literally "Peace be upon you", the traditional Muslim greeting, offered when Muslims meet each other.

Wa 'Alaykum as-Salam
"Peace be upon you too", is the reply to the greeting, expressing their mutual love, sincerity and best wishes.

Al-Hamdulillah
Literally "Praise be to Allah". It is used for expressing thanks and gratefulness to Allah. This supplication is also used when one sneezes, in order to thank Allah for having relieved discomfort out of His boundless mercy.

Subhanallah
Literally "Glory be to Allah". It reflects a Muslim's appreciation and amazement at observing any manifestation of Allah's greatness.

Insha' Allah
Literally "If Allah so wishes". Used by Muslims to indicate their decision to do something, provided they get help from Allah. It is recommended that whenever Muslims resolve to do something and make a promise, they should add "Insha' Allah".

Jazak Allah
Literally means: "May Allah Reward you" while thanking someone. A Muslim prays that Allah may reward the benefactor.

Some information about
the Animals and Birds

Lourie
There are many species of lourie birds. Some louries are found in dry regions. Some species are found in lush forested areas, and these louries have beautiful red wings. All louries have crests on top of their heads. They eat fruit and seeds.

Bushbuck
The bushbuck is a very shy antelope. It likes to live where the undergrowth is thick and dense. They eat seedpods, twigs, shoots, leaves, wild fruits and roots.

Hyena
Hyenas are native to Southern Asia and Africa. They are carnivores, which means they eat meat and carrion. They have very powerful jaws; this enables them to crack open bones. Female hyenas bear two to four young each season. They live for about 15 to 25 years.

Elephant
There are African elephants and Indian elephants. Of the two the African elephant is the largest, it is the largest land mammal in the world. They live to approximately 60 years of age. They like to live in large herds. Elephants eat leaves, shoots, grass, bark and berries, which makes them strictly vegetarian.

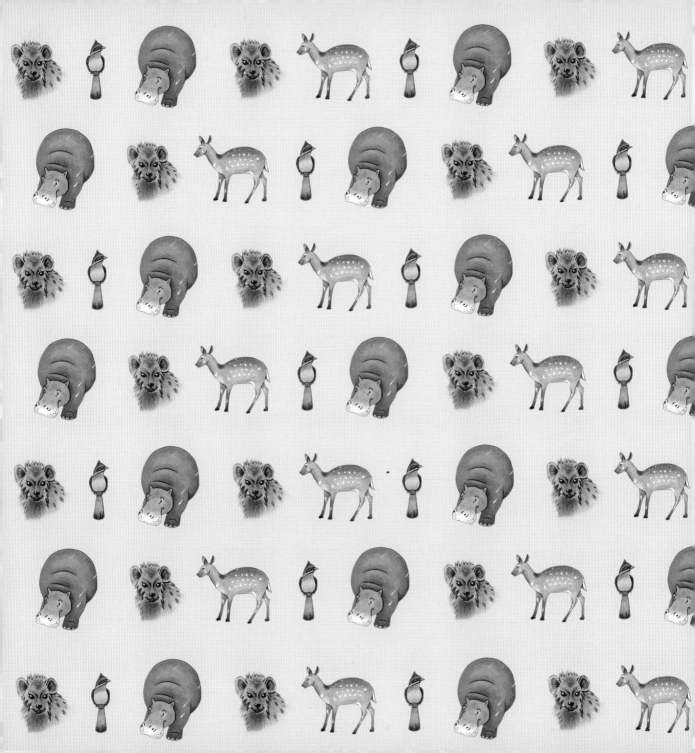